LIZARD BOY TALES

BY

MICHAEL POWER

LIZARD BOY TALES

Copyright © 2018 by Michael Power

ISBN 9798666493922

Printed in England

Michael is not a writer and was never an aspiring author until a surprise diagnosis of a critical illness. He then put pen to paper to prove that absolutely anyone can write a book of some kind.

To Ali, Edward & Jessica.

Prologue

The Marlow family lived in a town called Marlow, which was nothing more than a big coincidence and a bit confusing. Apart from that they were completely average.

They lived in an average sized house with an average sized garden, but they were lucky to live very close to a park with a great play area and some good trees for climbing.

Mr. Marlow worked a few days a week in London and the rest of the time he worked from an office in their home which was really just a big shelf. It had a printer balanced precariously on one end, his laptop in the middle and a pile of books and folders on the other end. He had a wonky stool to sit on and under the shelf was a big spaghetti like tangle of wires. He did something in marketing, but the kids didn't really know exactly what it was.

Mrs. Marlow made stuff for people. Curtains, cushions and the occasional wedding dress. She made everything with great pride and precision. She loved the house to be neat, but Ed, Jess and Mr. Marlow were all very untidy.

Ed was 11 and spent way too much time gaming. His 10-year-old sister Jess loved gaming too but they both loved the outdoors.

When they went on holiday to the seaside in Devon or Cornwall, they spent all day bodyboarding,

snorkeling and searching rock pools.

They were lucky because one set of grandparents lived in Cornwall and another lived in Devon.

The town of Marlow was a very long way from the sea, but it had a river running through the town and the fields next to the river were full of bugs, frogs, toads and even grass snakes so it was great for exploring when Ed and Jess got bored with computer games.

Ed and Jess went to the same school which was just a 10-minute walk from their house. Jess loved school. Ed wasn't so sure.

Chapter 1
School

Ed stared out of the window. He stared at the school field and the woods beyond.

He didn't care much for school – even on normal days. He didn't get it.

They did French lessons, but he'd been to France once and everyone he met spoke English. As for Maths, what was the point of knowing you're nine times table when you could use a calculator or the calculator app on your phone?

But that attitude had got him into trouble. In his recent maths homework he had a sheet of questions about shopping.

Q1: Oranges are 50p each. Apples are 30p each.

You buy 3 oranges and 6 apples.

How much change would you get from £5.00?

A: My Dad always uses a debit card - so I don't need to worry about change.

.........had been Ed's honest and considered answer and as far as he was concerned the same answer applied to the following nine questions.

Science was OK; you got to burn stuff and make things. Art was a laugh – he was good at that. He was OK at ball sports; good enough to get by and he held the school record for the standing long jump.

Ed's teachers all said the same thing. Good kid. Well behaved, good sense of humour but a bit of a chatterbox and very low concentration levels.

If he found it hard to concentrate on a normal day, today was a trillion, billion, google, gazillion times harder. And if there was such a number you could times it by nine to make use of the stupid times table.

His head was so full of stuff.

As he looked out, he saw a line of younger kids following the path towards the science block. At the front of the line was his sister Jess. She loved school.

She was the class representative on the school council. Jess was also a pretty cool sister. They had the odd disagreement but most of the time they got on brilliantly.

As Jess got closer Ed put his hand up to give her a quick wave. Jess spotted him. She put her thumb and finger together, drew them across her lips, smiled and carried on leading her classmates along the path. It was a sign that her lips were sealed so their secret was safe. At least that was a slight relief.

He took a deep breath.

"Ouch!!!"

He felt a sharp pain on his ankle.

He glanced across the table to see whether it was Mo or Will who had kicked him. Will was staring at him. Ed sensed it was a warning. He looked quizzically back at Will who leant his head slightly in the direction of Miss Frost.

"Well Edward" demanded Miss Frost "can you give me your answer?"

As he hadn't even heard the question it was going to be a problem.

In fact, he couldn't even remember what the lesson was. If it was Mr Bunsen at the front of the room it was science.

If it was Miss De Bus is was French.

The trouble with Miss Frost was that she took Maths

but also filled in any time another teacher was off sick. She had a very traditional approach. She had been at the school for nearly 40 years and had even taught Ed's Dad. She loved teaching or at least she loved proving how clever she was, she loved the clever kids and she loved proving that the day-dreamers would never make anything of their lives.

Ed daren't say he hadn't heard the question. Far better to have a go with a massive guess and hope for the best.

In maths they were still working on the nine times table

Miss Frost wouldn't ask an easy question. Ed knew that 54 was in there somewhere. It was as good a guess as any.

"Urm, I think it's, urm 54 Miss"

Mo was already trying not to laugh but the answer forced the laugh out of his nose resulting in a huge snot bubble.

That set the whole class off.

"Silence!!!!!" screamed Miss Frost "you will all be silent"

As 30 kids desperately suppressed giggles Miss Frost walked slowly towards Ed and leant on the edge of the table.

"So, let me be clear Edward Marlow" She leaned closer.

"The question was - in the book 'James and the Giant Peach' apart from James, which is your favorite character and why?' Your answer is 54!!!!!!"

Ed tried to save the situation "Urm, I meant to say The Centipede he's like, seriously cool and proper funny"

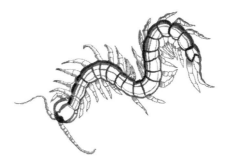

That was too much for the class. They exploded into fits of laughter.

"Quiet, quiet!!!" Miss Frost yelled again "Edward Marlow, go and stand out in the corridor... the rest of you will all be in detention unless I have total silence right now!!!"

Ed escaped a trip to the Headmasters office. He got a proper telling off and a Friday lunchtime detention. Miss Frost reminded him that he was a dreamer and that no good would come of him unless he changed his attitude and that in her day, he'd have been in detention every day for a week blah blah blah blah. He looked straight at her nodded a lot and said sorry a lot.

He went to the lunch break. Mo and Will were waiting. "That was epic dude" said Mo and put his hand up.

Ed shook his head, but he couldn't help smiling. He high-fived Mo and Will.

"Not as epic as your snot bubble" laughed Ed "it was melon- sized"

"Seriously Ed, are you OK?" asked Will "it's like you're in another world?"

"Yeah I'm OK"

Ed tucked into his sandwiches - and thought back through the events of the last few weeks.

Chapter 2
Where the trouble began

Two weeks earlier Ed was having the best time of his life. At the end of the long Summer school break Ed, Jess, their Mum, Dad, Nan and Grandad Bunn (Flora and John) had been on holiday.

They were on the island of Madeira which was apparently part of Portugal. Although Portuguese was the official language of Madeira everyone spoke good English which further confirmed Ed's opinion that learning foreign languages was a waste of time.

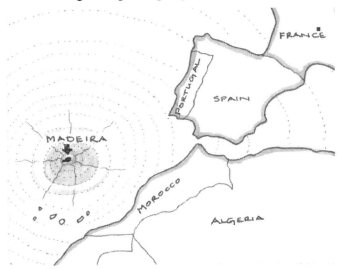

Getting to Madeira had been fun. They had to wake up super-early to get to Bristol Airport. At the airport their Mum was very well organised. She had a bag with all the passports, tickets, flight details and information about the hotel ready for when they arrived in Madeira. Their Dad was less well organised. He spent most of the time complaining about queues and other passengers saying things like "how can they possibly be allowed to take a suitcase that big on the plane? It should be in the luggage compartment"

When they went through the final security check there was a hold up as a guy had walked off without his laptop. When he finally came back to collect it there was more confusion over his flight details.

Mr. Marlow turned to Jess and Ed and said " I think he forgot to check his brain in when he got to the airport" Ed and Jess laughed but Mrs Marlow overheard and gave Mr. Marlow a friendly shove and a stare. The same stare she used on the kids when they hadn't cleaned their rooms or finished their homework. "It's like I've got three children here, will you please behave!" she whispered

Mr. Marlow just grinned and nodded.

After what seemed like forever, they boarded the plane and the excitement grew as the holiday really seemed to have started.

The flight was fun and not too long. Looking down at the clouds from above was awesome. It looked like you could just walk straight across them, a bright white, marsh-mallow wonderland. It was a laugh looking for shapes in the clouds too. Some looked like dragons, some like cartoon human faces others like pigs, dolphins and birds. Jess kept saying she could see unicorn and lama shapes, but Ed kept saying "Nah, they don't look anything like it"

After they landed Mr. Marlow went back into his joke moany mood. One of the other passengers who had taken a massive piece of hand-luggage on to the plane was having all of her cases fully searched which seemed to make Mr. Marlow very happy.

Pretty soon they were on a minibus and after a short and very speedy ride, during which Mrs. Marlow asked the driver if he thought he was a Formula One Racing Driver, they arrived at the hotel.

The grandparents had arrived already and were waiting for them as the minibus pulled in.   Mrs. Marlow was relieved to get out of the minibus in one piece. Mr. Marlow was happily chatting to the driver and asking if he was available for hire in case the family wanted to take a trip around the island " Is it OK if I call you Lewis?" asked Mr. Marlow. The driver looked a bit confused. He pointed to a badge on his jacket which had the name "Tiago" printed on it but before he could speak Mr. Marlow continued " I know, I know, your name is Tiago but I'll call you Lewis, like Lewis Hamilton the racing driver. You know" he said and then pretended to hold a steering wheel and made some zooming car engine noises. The driver nodded and smiled as he passed his business card to Mr. Marlow. Ed and Jess grimaced and looked at each other. Parents were soooo embarrassing.

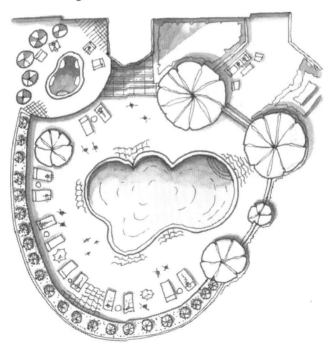

Their Nan and Grandad came down to help them with their luggage. There was a lot of hugging and conversations about the journey. Ed and Jess followed. They were trying to be polite, but they were desperate to get in the pool. What made it worse was the fact that the reception area of the hotel had huge windows which looked out over the hotel grounds. The pool looked amazing.

Ed's grandparents had a thing called a time-share which Ed and Jess didn't really understand. They had a big apartment on the 5th floor of a hotel which they could use for 4 weeks every year and other people could use it for the rest of the time. Basically, it meant they were staying in an epic hotel with a massive swimming pool. Unlike the pools they visited back in the UK this one wasn't just an oblong. It had all sorts of curves and even a little bridge over one of the narrow sections.

They checked into the hotel and were directed to the lifts at the far end of the reception area.

Mrs. Marlow sensed how excited the kids were. "Tell you what" she said "I've got your swimming gear in my hand luggage, as soon as we get to the room you can get changed and head for the pool with Dad. I'll unpack quickly and I'll be down in a few minutes"

The lift door started to open. Jess dodged round Ed and ran towards the lift. There was a strange boinging sound as she bounced back into the reception area and landed on a sofa.

The lift was full of people heading to the pool. Most of them were carrying huge inflatables. Jess had rebounded off an exceptionally large, blow-up, rainbow-coloured unicorn.

She was too excited to be embarrassed even though everyone was laughing. As soon as the lift was empty, they piled in. Mr. Marlow pressed the button for the 5th floor, and they were on their way.

Chapter 3
Lizards.

Soon the whole family were round the pool.

Ed quickly spotted something else which was pretty awesome.

Ed loved lizards. He'd never seen one in the UK. There was a low wall all around the hotel complex and it was covered in them. They weren't massive the biggest were about 15cm long. Most were brown but some were bright green, and a few were a grey-blue colour. On the first day he came close to catching a couple, but they were quick!

On the second morning they all headed straight down to the pool after breakfast. It was already really hot. Ed and Jess jumped straight in. After a while they heard Mrs. Marlow calling them, she had bought everyone ice creams and lollies so they gathered around the sun-loungers. Ed couldn't resist trying to catch a lizard. He was getting closer every time he tried. He made a grab for one and just missed it.

"You'll need to be quicker than that" his Nan said, laughing.

Ed smiled and wandered back to perch on the edge of his Nan's sunbed. Before he got there, he looked up at Jess. She had a mouth full of orange lolly, but she was pointing at the wall. Ed looked back. As he'd tried to catch the first lizard a dollop of ice-cream had dripped onto the wall. In seconds it was surrounded by hungry, thirsty reptiles. So, it seemed ice-cream was good bait.

Ed crept over to the wall. The lizards were distracted by the sticky, sugary liquid as the ice-cream melted. He crept up slowly and quietly. He grabbed one.

Got it!

Or at least had it.

Ed was sure he'd caught the lizard, but it somersaulted into the flowers at the base of the wall and vanished.

He realised immediately what had happened.

Lizards shed their tails when they're attacked. It's a great survival tactic and the remaining tail soon heals over and grows back a bit. The bit of the tail that drops off flicks around for a while to distract whatever is attacking the lizard.

Ed could feel the tail in his hand. He walked back to the family.

"Don't tell me you caught one" said his Nan, seeing Ed with his hand clasped tight shut.

"Not exactly" he replied, suppressing a smile.

"I don't want a lizard anywhere near me" his Nan added, lifting her ice-cream safely away and edging back on her sunbed.

Ed opened his hand.

The tail was still wriggling.

"Eeuuww !!!" shouted Jess "...that's disgusting"

His Nan leant forward nervously but as she did the tail flicked and landed on her lap.

She screamed.

She jumped up.

Her ice-cream flew in the air over the newspaper of the man on the next-door sunbed and landed with a plop.

He calmly pulled down his paper. The ice-cream tub was stuck on the top of his head like a miniature hat. The melting ice-cream ran down his face. Two of the cherries from the top of the tub had slid down his sunglasses, one on each lens. He looked like a cream - covered, cross-eyed clown.

The Marlow family froze, staring at the poor man

Mrs. Marlow and Nan Bunn started to apologise profusely both grabbing towels to show that they were willing to clean the mess up.

Fortunately, the man's wife saw the funny side.

"Shame I didn't get that on video – it would have been great on YouTube"

As he wiped the melting ice cream from his face, he managed a smile

"I needed to cool down but that wasn't what I had in mind"

Ed was told to apologise. He didn't really see why. It wasn't his fault, but it was one of those occasions when he knew it could have been a lot worse, so he mumbled

"Sorry".

A couple more days of sun. Ed and Jess were getting pretty good at catching lizards – they ended up with just a tail a few times but they caught plenty and had cut the top of a huge water bottle to keep the lizards in for a while to watch them more closely.

On the fifth day Mr. and Mrs. Marlow started talking about the weather. Grown-ups always love talking about the weather.

The specific topic was the rain which was on the way. Heavy rain and storms were forecast. Everyone was saying how unusual it was to have rain in Madeira at that time of year.

The forecast was right.

They woke up on the sixth day of the holiday to the most amazing rain. Huge heavy drops crashing down.

It was a day to stay in the hotel. The hotel games-room kept Ed and Jess occupied for a while.

They had a game of table-tennis. Neither of them knew the rules but it was pretty funny smashing the ball around the room in the general direction of the table. The fun ended when Jess accidently wacked the ball straight at Ed's head. Ed swung the bat up to protect his face. He connected with the ball. It rocketed upwards and wedged into a beam in the ceiling. They stared at the ball, then at each other then they both fell over laughing. They tried to reach the ball with a snooker cue but it was no good, so they trooped back to the room. The TV in the hotel room had plenty of channels including one which was just cartoons so they watched that for most of the afternoon. Even that got a bit boring.

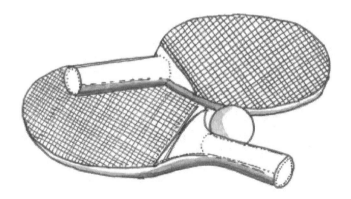

"Can we go swimming?" asked Jess

"Not today" said Mrs Marlow "let's hope the rain passes and we'll do something cool tomorrow"

Chapter 4
The Rain

The next day the rain was even harder and the palm trees around the pool, swayed like long-haired street - dancers.

More cartoons.

By lunch time the next day Mr. Marlow had had enough!

"Let's go down to the pool – we'll get soaked on the way but we're going in the pool anyway so what's the worst that could happen?"

Mrs. Marlow wasn't so sure.

"Be careful – it's so windy and they're forecasting thunder. A swimming pool is one of the worst places to be if there's lightening around"

"Not as bad as standing on top of a really tall building holding a long metal pole" Jess chimed in.

"Right" said Mrs Marlow patiently "but on the grounds that we're not asking you to go up to the hotel roof with a long metal pole I still don't think it's a good idea"

"We'll be alright" insisted Mr. Marlow, already getting his stuff together. "If there's even a hint of thunder and lightening we'll come straight back in"

They were the only people around the pool. No one else was daft enough.

The pool was weird. The water felt really warm. The rain was so hard it made an amazing hissing sound. As the drops bounced up from the water surface they collided with other drops and it created an odd mist which rose about 30 cm.

Being underwater watching the drops crash through the surface was epic too. It looked like a gazillion tiny blue bullets being fired into the pool.

It was great to be out of the room but all too soon Dad was calling them.

"Nearly dinner time guys, let's get back to the room".

He had pulled two sunshades together to provide a bit of shelter from the rain.

"Not much point in getting dry" said Ed, wrapping a

towel around himself "we'll be wet again by the time we get to the hotel doors"

As he grudgingly dried himself Ed noticed something. A group of large lizards.

They were near a huge hotel sign which sat on posts sticking up from the low wall. The sign provided a sheltered spot on the wall and a few good-sized lizards were taking advantage.

Ed could pretty much reach them without completely leaving the protection of the sunshades.

He reached for the nearest one.

He grabbed it.

There was a massive bang.

The next thing he knew he was looking up at his Dad. Everything was hazy. He could just about see that his Dad's mouth was moving but he couldn't hear anything. His ears were ringing. Slowly the words became clearer.

"Ed, Ed, mate please say you're OK, Ed can you hear me?"

Ed could hear Jess crying. "Ed are you OK?"

"I think so "

"Does anything hurt?"

"Errmm kind of – I feel really fizzy"

"Don't move Ed; Jess he's OK don't worry."

Ed was aware that other faces were appearing. The pool attendant was looking very concerned and was on his mobile. One of the receptionists was holding an umbrella over him

Ed was also aware that he had something in his hand. It was a Lizards tail. He slowly and gently popped it into the pocket of his swimming shorts.

Ed tried to sit up, but his Dad told him not to move.

"You got struck by lightning Ed" Jess shouted, happy that her brother seemed OK.

He looked across to the Hotel Sign which was smashed and blackened. It seemed a long way away.

"Ed, it was amazing, there was a massive flash and you just flew through the air"

"I don't feel too amazing" he grumbled.

The paramedics soon arrived – checking his pulse, asking him what hurt. They decided it would be best to take him to hospital to do some proper checks.

By now Mrs Marlow had arrived and as you can imagine she wasn't happy with Mr Marlow.

"What did I tell you?" she demanded.

Mr Marlow looked down and mumbled that he was sorry "The main thing is he's OK" he added.

Jess decided to have her say too.

"Well Mummy, you said the swimming pool was the worst place to be but Ed was out of the pool when the lightening struck he was right over there by the....." before she could finish she realised her mum was giving her one of those looks which meant "Are you sure you want to argue with me right now?"

There was only room for one extra person in the ambulance. Mrs Marlow insisted on going with Ed.

"I'll call you as soon as we get there" she shouted as the doors closed and the ambulance raced off.

As it turned out Ed was OK. He went back to the hotel and the last few days of the holiday were great. Ed was a bit of a celebrity. All the staff and most of the guests had heard about the incident. Everywhere Jess and Ed went the staff patted them on the head. They got free drinks and ice-cream at the poolside and were generally well looked after.

Chapter 5
Home Trouble

By the time they got home Ed felt totally normal. He was even looking forward to going back to school to tell his mates about the holiday.

He started to unpack his case. His mum had asked him to make sure all his pockets were empty. Ed loved picking up everything; conkers, shells, unusual stones; pretty much anything he found. It meant that the Marlow's washing machine broke down a lot. The repair man would always finish the job and appear with a handful of elastic bands, marbles, feathers and acorns.

Ed took out his swimming shorts – to his surprise there was a lizard's tail. It must be the one he'd grabbed before the lightning strike. It was something else to show his mates at school. As he looked closer it seemed to move slightly. He stared at it but it didn't move again. He had a plastic tub of stuff on his windowsill. Batteries, coins, a few fossils, a shark's tooth, paper clips – he put the tail in for safe-keeping while he carried on with his unpacking

Next morning Ed looked in the tub. The tail was definitely moving, and it was bigger than he remembered. As he put his hand in to pick it up his finger touched one of the coins. He pulled his hand out quickly – the coin was hot. He realised that the batteries and the coins had formed a kind of electrical circuit. That got him thinking. He'd had a clip together circuit board as part of a science kit for his birthday.

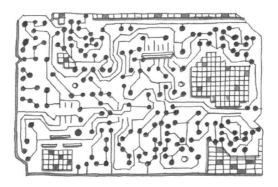

He put the kit together. The tail was slightly curved, but he unfurled a couple of paperclips to hold it in place. He flicked the switch which made the tail move slightly. He took another paperclip and as he straightened it his mum called him. He was concentrating so hard it made him jump. The end of the clip jabbed into his finger. It started to bleed.

His mum called again.

He would have to carry on after breakfast. He ate at a superspeed rate. He wanted to get back upstairs and quickly but his mum made him slow down – risk of indigestion!

After what felt like an hour he ran back upstairs. His room was a real mess, well even messier than usual.

He was fairly sure he hadn't left it quite that bad and Jess had been with him having breakfast, so it wasn't her.

He bent down to get under his bed to carry on with the experiment.

What he saw stopped him his tracks. He was frozen to the spot. Mouth wide open. He pinched the skin on his arm to check that he was awake and not in the middle of some epic dream. It wasn't a dream

There on the floor, lying curled up on top of the circuit board was.....him. A naked full-size boy who

looked exactly like Ed.

"Dude, can you, like, help me up, this is seriously uncomfortable."

Ed stepped forward to help the boy out from under his bed. The boy turned around. Ed realised that the tail was still attached to the circuit board and still very much attached to the boy. Ed removed the paperclips. Somehow the electrical charge combined with drops of blood from Ed's finger had created a full-sized lookalike. Ed's mind was whirring. Perhaps the lightening strike back in Madeira had affected the tail. He definitely had it in his hand at the time.

They stood looking at each other for a few seconds. "Any chance of borrowing some clothes, I'm freezing"

Ed grabbed a pair of shorts and a sweatshirt. The boy put them on.

This was beyond weird. "Who are you?" asked Ed.

"Not sure dude, I think I'm.....you"

There was a mirror on the wardrobe door. They stood side by side looking at their reflection.

Ed heard footsteps on the stairs. "Quick" he said.

Before the boy could respond Ed bundled him into the wardrobe.

"Keep quiet" he whispered.

"Who are you talking to Ed?" asked Jess.

"Don't just barge into my room"

"Ooooh stresssyyyy!!!"

"Jess, something weird has happened, it's the weirdest most epic thing times a gazillion but you have to keep a secret"

Jess could tell he was serious, so she nodded.

"Promise?" said Ed

"I promise"

Ed opened the wardrobe - Jess screamed.

Ed slammed the wardrobe shut.

Jess stood and stared at the closed wardrobe. Ed put his fingers to his lips.

Jess nodded

Ed opened the wardrobe again Jess screamed even louder

Ed slammed the door again.

"What's going on?" shouted Mum

"Nothing" replied Jess "just messing around"

"Well try to keep the noise down a bit, and no more screaming!"

"OK mum!" Ed and Jess shouted in unison.

Ed nodded at Jess.

Jess took a deep breath and nodded back.

Ed opened the door again

The boy stepped out.

"Who are you??"

The boy smiled and shrugged.

Ed told Jess what had happened, now they had to decide what to do next.

Could they tell mum and dad?

What could they call the boy?

Where could he sleep?

What would he eat?

This was going to get interesting

"You're going to have to hide in here until we can figure out what to do" said Ed.

At lunchtime Ed and Jess managed to put food in their pockets without Mrs. Marlow noticing.

Up in the room the boy didn't look too impressed as they emptied the squashed potatoes and lumps of chicken onto a plate from Jessica's toy kitchen collection.

Then they all started giggling.

"Thanks guys, this is.......urrmm, awesome!"

They managed to make a hidden den under Ed's cabin bed but they knew he couldn't stay there forever.

Chapter 6

Back to now

Ed got through the rest of the school day.

He and Jess sat in silence in the car on the way back from school.

They were both thinking the same thing. Would the boy still be there?

He was.

"What are we going to do?" he asked "I've been totally bored today"

Ed had been thinking. They had to tell mum.

Mum got stressed about small stuff, leaving dirty socks in the middle of the bedroom floor, not putting your hand over your mouth when you sneezed, not flushing the loo or leaving muddy footprints in the hall.

But when big stuff happened - when the washing machine exploded and flooded the kitchen, when a storm caused a tree branch to crash through the living room window, she knew what to do.

Mum was cool.

Mum knew how to handle a crisis. Mum always knew what to say and do.

Mum was calm under pressure

Ed called for mum to come upstairs

Mum saw the boy.

Mum fainted.

"Well, that could have gone better" said Ed as he hurried to the bathroom to get his mum a glass of water.

He got back to the room. His mum was already sitting up. She thanked Ed for the water and got to her feet, took a deep breath and regained her composure.

Ed went through the story again. "So, you're Ted"

"I guess so" replied Ted, shrugging his shoulders.

"Right – so you've been here for two days" "Yep"

"Have you had anything to eat?"

"Kind of – some dry chicken, squashed potatoes, an apple and a bag of jelly babies"

"OK" said mum "anyone for Pizza"

"Yeah cool" the three all shouted at the same time.

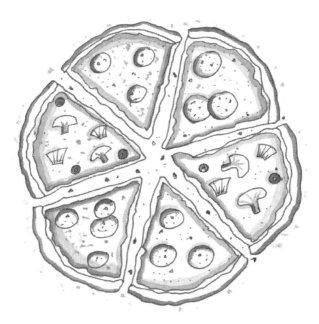

While they ate their tea, Mum phoned Dad to prepare him for what he would come home to.

Not long after they heard Dad's key in the door.

Mum met him in the hall. The kids could hear frantic whispering but couldn't hear what was being said.

They carried on with their Pizza.

Mr Marlow's head appeared around the corner of the kitchen then disappeared. There was more whispering.

Mr. and Mrs. Marlow came in together.

"Hi guys" said Dad, acting as if everything was normal "Hi Ted"

"Hi Dad!" they called out together.

So, the Marlow's suddenly had three kids including an instant 11 year old who was an exact copy of Ed.

They needed to get organised.

The next day Ed and Jess went to school as normal. Mr Marlow took them in and stayed to meet the head mistress. He managed to persuade her that his nephew, Ted, was staying with them while his parents were helping to build a school in Africa. The project had over run, and they couldn't get back so Ted would be staying with the Marlows for a while.

Meanwhile Mum took Ted into town. Ed hated having his hair cut so he had a huge mop of blonde hair.

Ted was given a very sharp hair cut – he looked

different already.

Ed wore glasses Ted hopefully wouldn't need them. They'd need to wear the same uniform to school but with different clothes outside school they might get away without too many questions

Chapter 7
Dog Trouble

The Marlow's lived near a big park which was great – what wasn't so great was that it was popular with dog owners and their dogs. When he was four years old Ed had been bundled over by an excited Labrador which had proceeded to burst his Spiderman football. Ever since he'd been scared of dogs.

There were houses with dogs down their road. Mr Marlow said that only one of them was a real dog – a Jack Russell. The others were crossbreeds. Bingo at number 8 was a cross between a Labrador and a poodle and his owner loved to explain that the dog was a labradoodle.

At number 20 was a cross between a cocker spaniel and a poodle - a "cockapoo" called Hector

Just around the corner was a massive beast called Tyson belonging to Philbert Bland. Tyson was massive - a cross between a Bull Mastiff and a Poodle.

He was huge and so were his poos. Philbert Bland was one of those owners who carried plastic bags to pick up his dog's droppings but only if he thought people were watching. Otherwise he left them, but no other dog was capable of such steaming piles.They were bigger than some of the dogs in the park.

 Mr Marlow, fed up with cleaning dog muck from Ed's trainers, said that Tyson's specific breed should be called "A Bull Massive Poo"

It was early Saturday morning and the kids were heading for the park to kick a ball around. Mr Marlow said he'd pop to the corner shop to grab some drinks and catch up with them.

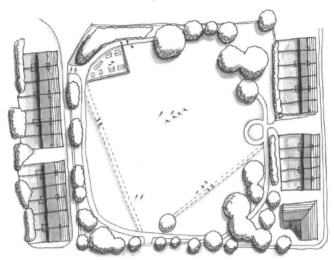

They were the only ones at the park and they started a kick about.

After a couple of minutes Tyson appeared, followed closely by Philbert Bland.

"Aww Mannnn" groaned Ed.

"What's the problem?" asked Ted.

"It's that stupid dog – quick grab the ball".

Tyson squatted down to do his business.

Philbert Bland waited patiently. He'd hoped that no one would be in the park this early, but he would have no choice but to clear up.

As soon as Tyson had 'finished', he saw the kids and bounded towards them.

Jess squealed.

"He just wants to play" shouted Philbert Bland, trying to remove a plastic bag from his pocket and hold onto the extendable lead at the same time.

The ball was still on the floor. Ted stepped forward to pick it up.

Tyson came to a sudden stop about 10 meters away. He crouched slightly and growled but the growl turned into a whimper.

Somewhere deep inside his animal instincts stirred. To everyone else Ted looked like a perfectly normal 11-year-old kid. To Tyson he looked like a giant lizard. Even with his size - Tyson was scared. For the first time in his life he was genuinely scared.

Philbert, who was still bending over to clear up the huge poo, glanced up. Ted took a step forward to pick the ball up. Tyson freaked out. With another loud whimper he turned tail and took off as fast as he could.

"Tyson" cried Philbert Bland " what's the................ matttersraaarrrghh!!"

Tyson shot passed his owner who was clinging grimly to the lead. The dog's momentum span him round and he landed face down as the lead was finally ripped from his grasp.

The dog didn't look back. He headed towards the far

entrance of the park with the lead bouncing after like a crazy kangaroo.

The kids stared in amazement as the dog disappeared through the gap in the fence.

"Tysonnnnn" wailed Philbert Bland.

Chapter 8

Sirens

There was a screech of breaks from the road on the other side of the hedge, followed by a loud bang – then silence. Philbert Bland was still lying face down. He was large, very unfit and was struggling to get to his feet. He finally drew himself up and took a couple of steps forwards.

As he did Tyson came back through the park entrance.

"Oh, thank goodness!" Philbert exclaimed "here Tyson, here boy!"

He soon realised that Tyson was straining at his lead. Two seconds later a huge tattooed gentleman with a shaved head appeared at the other end of the lead.

"This yours????" he growled.

"Urrrmmm well ....urrr yes it is, is he OK"

"He's fine" grumbled the man "which is more that can be said for my van!"

The man was followed by a disheveled cyclist in a full Lycra body suit and helmet who, in turn, was followed by an old lady.

"This creature knocked this bloke of his bike. I swerved to miss him and hit this lady's car"

"This is going to cost you – I need your name and address for the insurance and..... pwoar.....what's that pong?"

Philbert Bland was suddenly aware of the smell too.

He looked down – he had a massive pizza-shaped poo patch on his jumper.

They all heard the sound of sirens.

Two policewomen came into the far entrance of the park. At the same time Ed, Ted and Jess heard Mr Marlow's concerned voice calling.

"You all OK??"

"Yep – we're all fine" shouted Jess, putting both thumbs up for confirmation.

"What's going on??"

"No idea.... the dog just totally freaked out" said Jess.

By now the two policewomen were trying to take down Philbert's details – both standing a few feet away from him with their hands over their noses.

Philbert looked totally miserable.

"You can go now "said one of the officers "but we'll be in touch soon"

The man with the van stood and glared at Philbert as he walked away with his head down. Tyson sloped along next to him, ears down, tail between his legs.

Jess told Mr. Marlow the whole story – he couldn't help but smile when he heard about the poo on the jumper. "At least now he'll know what it's like to clear up after that dog of his!"

"C'mon guys... lets go and grab a drink – anyone fancy a hot chocolate and a cake?"

As they walked along the path to the gates on the other side of the park. Mr. Marlow strode ahead and spotted their neighbor, Major Franklyn Gunn approaching with his dog Bullet. The Major had retired from the Army many years before, but he was always dressed immaculately and wore his regimental tie. His tightly curled grey hair and beard stood out against his dark brown skin.

His dog, Bullet, was a Jack Russel. When he was a puppy Bullet had been, slim, copper-coloured and superfast so the name fitted him well. 14 years later he was greyer than copper, much slower and heavier. He looked more like a cannon ball than a bullet.

Mr. Marlow had never been in the Armed Forces but he and the Major always greeted each other with a salute and a big smile.

"What's going on over there?" Asked the Major.

"Not really too sure" replied Mr. Marlow "Philbert's dog ripped the lead out of his hand and caused a bit of a prang on the road outside. No one got hurt. The kids seem to think something freaked the dog out, but they don't know what it was"

By now the kids had caught up. The Major pulled on Bullets lead but Bullet was trying desperately to dig his claws into the concrete on the path. The Major looked down, slightly puzzled.

"Come along Bullet"

Bullet wasn't coming willingly, just skidding along the path as the Major pulled on his lead. Bullet's eyesight wasn't so good, but his instincts were still sharp. He was suddenly all too aware of Ted. He could see the normal outline of a human but like Tyson a few minutes earlier, he was petrified as his primal fears told him this was no ordinary person. By now Ted was very close. Bullet, realising he couldn't grip the path or turn and run suddenly took a few scampering steps in front of his owner and made a vertical leap into a bin on the side of the path.

Everyone stared at the bin.

"I haven't seen him move like that for ten years" exclaimed the puzzled Major.

Mr. Marlow stepped forward to pull the poor pooch out of the bin, but Bullet was just digging deeper down through the rubbish. "Kids- carry on and find a table in the Café - I'll be along in a minute. A few seconds after they'd left, Bullet relaxed and Mr. Marlow and the Major managed to pull him out. At first, they both took a deep breath but soon realised that what they feared was blood was just ketchup from an old burger. Closer investigation showed he was fine albeit a bit smelly and with a few other sauces, mustard and mayonnaise dotted around his back and belly.

"Well, I must say, that was most peculiar behaviour" said the Major, stroking his beard thoughtfully.

Mr. Marlow was using his hanky to get the worst of the mess out of the dog's hair.

"Please don't worry" added the Major "I'll take him straight back home. I think he's had enough excitement"

"If you're sure Major" Mr. Marlow replied "I'll leave you to it and I'll catch up with the kids. I'm really sorry about all this"

"Nothing for you to be sorry about. It's just all very odd" Said the Major as he gave a salute and a big smile.

Mr. Marlow saluted back and hurried off to catch up with the kids in the café.

The Major looked back thoughtfully stroking his neat grey beard for a few seconds before starting his short march home, the bedraggled Bullet shuffling sadly behind.

Chapter 9
Philbert Bland

Philbert Bland, now back home, lived with his mum. Although he was over 50 years old he had always lived at home - he was a strange character.

At school he had been a bit of a loner. He couldn't see the point of sport so at break times, when all the other kids were playing football or chase, he stayed inside with a book. And then something happened. The school got its first computer. It seems strange to think about it now, but it was a pretty big deal in 1977.

In fact, the school got three computers. The maths teacher set up a computer club. It was nine kids crowded round three dark green screens with light green letters and numbers flashing across them.

It seemed a million years away from Ipads and lap-tops but at the time it was amazing and Philbert loved it. He got to know everything about them. Gradually the group got smaller – just three of them - which meant he got a computer to himself.

The maths teacher even let him take one home during the holidays. He told him that in America people were making careers out of the new technology.

Some guy called William Gates and a gang of other long-haired kids were writing computer languages and programmes which would change the world. Philbert was jealous of these kids in California. He would have loved to have friends who understood computers. He didn't get on with other kids, even the others in the computer club. They were nowhere near as clever as him.

When he left school, he worked for IBM – a massive computer company. Philbert knew about computers but he hated working with people, and he hated being told what to do. So, he left. He got other jobs, but he never found anyone who appreciated his brilliance. So Philbert spent most of his time at home playing with his computers.

As more people had access to computers – there were more complex computer breakdowns. Even though Philbert was difficult to deal with people started to ask him to fix their computers. So he got paid for sitting at home doing what he loved. He got so busy he built a big shed in his garden and filled it with all the technology he needed.

 Then a shop selling and repairing computers set up in the high street: "Can Do Computers" They sent their really difficult jobs to Philbert - the stuff "Can Do" couldn't do. That meant he only had to deal with one person – the shop owner, and that suited him fine. His mum cooked his meals and he had Tyson for company.

All the kids he'd heard about in America and the other kids in his old school computer club were all multi- millionaires by now.

Philbert was quietly angry with the world for not allowing him to make the best of his skills. He was surrounded by idiots.

Chapter 10
Cat Trouble

Mrs Henman lived at the end of the road. She was extremely tall and very elegant. She had a cat called Queeny. Mrs Henman had an old bike with a basket on the front and everywhere she went she took Queeny who sat in the basket. Mrs Henman put a small pink scarf around Queeny's neck. As Mrs Henman cycled along, sitting very upright, people she passed would "Oooh" and "Ahhh" at the sight of the cat wearing the bow.

Mrs Henman pretended not to notice but she swelled with pride every time it happened and Queeny had the look of a very regal, immensely proud animal.

Today the pair were on their usual Saturday morning circuit around the town. It was a beautiful sunny day so there were plenty of people out and about to admire them.

Ed, Ted, Jess and Dad were walking back from the park.

Mrs Henman peddled serenely towards them. Queeny suddenly felt very uneasy. She glanced in Ted's direction. She was a very fat pampered cat but somewhere deep inside she knew something was very wrong.

As they got closer to Ted, Queeny flattened her ears and hissed - but being in the basket meant she was moving unavoidably in Ted's direction. She needed to act. She jumped straight up. A Nano-second later she knew it was a mistake. Cats can usually land on their feet, but the momentum of the bike and the road surface below would mean a very bumpy landing.

So Queeny made a grab to save herself. The only thing to grab was Mrs Henman's head. With her front paws grasping the ridges in Mrs Henman helmet and her back paws clasped around her neck she clung on with all her strength.

Mrs Henman let out a scream which was muffled by a face full of feline fur.

The bike swerved across the road. It bumped up the curb and across the pavement.

Passers-by looked on in amazement as the bike disappeared through the open door of the Saucy Sardine Fish and Chip Shop, sending customers diving for cover. The bike came to a halt as it collided, relatively gently, with the counter and slid to the floor. Mrs Henman still gripping the handlebars - Queeny still gripping her helmet.

Realising she was on solid ground the cat let go and leapt to the floor. Still frightened she looked over her shoulder. Through the door she could see Ted.

She needed to get as far away as possible, so she took off around the counter, claws skittering on the polished floor and she disappeared into the store room at the back of the kitchen.

Confused people in the queue stepped forward to help Miss Henman untangle herself from the bike. One old man, sitting at his usual table was so surprised his false teeth fell out of his mouth onto his plate and into his mushy peas.

Alfredo the shop owner followed the cat. Queeny sat

in the furthest corner hissing.

Aflredo stood in the doorway – blocking the cat's exit route. When he lived back in Portugal, Aflredo had played in goal for his local team and even had trials for a top professional team, Benfica. However, 30 years of owning a fish and chip shop meant he had put on a fair bit of weight, but he still reckoned he had good reflexes.

He moved forward; legs slightly apart. His arms outstretched; almost as if he was about to face a penalty kick.

Queeny weighed up her options – her eyes were wide; her ears were flat against her head.

"Here kitty, it's OK. I won't hurt you, here kitty kitty"

Queeny made a break for it - she sprang to Alfredo's

right. He dived and reached for the cat. He got his fingertips to her, but it wasn't a clean catch – a bit like pushing a ball round the goalpost.

What he actually did was send Queeny spinning into a massive vat of freshly made batter.

"On no! It took me all morning to make zees batter."

By now Queeny had given up. Alfredo scooped the batter-soaked cat out of the vat. She looked a sorry sight.

Holding her at arms length he carried her back out into the shop.

Mrs Henman had never been so embarrassed. "Dees cat haz cost me lotta money miss" whispered Alfredo

"I'm so sorry she spluttered" grabbing a £10 note from her purse.

She righted her bike and carefully placed the still

dripping cat in the basket and shuffled out into the sunlight.

She started to cycle home with as much dignity as she could muster but everyone was staring, and plenty were laughing.

The Marlows hadn't seen the full incident and had continued the walk home. It was a stunningly hot day.

As they got to the end of their road Miss Henman was coming around the corner on her bike. The sun had hardened the batter. The family watched in puzzled amazement as Miss Henman removed what appeared to be a statue of a drowned cat from her basket. The only clue to the fact that Queeny was inside was a pair of crazed green eyes staring out through holes in the batter.

"Looks like catfish and chips for dinner" said Mr. Marlow quietly. The kids giggled.

It was a strange day and was about to get even more bizarre

Chapter 11
The Vets

Mrs Marlow opened the door to let Mr. Marlow and the kids in.

Jess couldn't wait to tell her mum about seeing Queeny all covered in what looked like batter.

"Did you offer to help?" Mrs Marlow asked her husband.

"No he didn't" interrupted Jess "but he did make a very funny joke about catfish and chips"

"Thanks Jess" replied Mr Marlow sarcastically "but I guess we should go and make sure she's OK. She doesn't have a car and the nearest vet's practice is five miles away.

They all walked round to Miss Henman's. When she opened the door, she was still in shock and through the hallway they could see Queeny, still solidly encased in batter, laying on the draining board near the sink.

"Are you OK?" asked Mr Marlow, softly.

Miss Henman didn't say anything - she just shook her head and pointed at Queeny.

"I... I...I...Don't know what to do" she whimpered.

"Well how about we give you and the cat a lift to the

vets and we can wait with you until we know it's OK?"

Miss Henman nodded and shuffled through to the kitchen.

She wrapped Queeny in an old towel and followed the Marlows as they walked to their car.

As they reached the car Mr Marlow turned to the kids. "You guys wait here and I'll........."

It was too late. They weren't going to miss this trip. They'd never had a pet so this would be a first and they were keen to find out what had happened to the cat.

After a few minutes in the car Miss Henman gradually lost the shocked look on her face. She was still waring her bike helmet, which was a bit odd, but they didn't want to tell her.

"She just j-j-j-jumped in the batter? Don't know why. The batter, she jumped in it, in the f-f-f-fish and chip shop; j-j- j-j- jumped on my head before that. Don't know why, don't know why"

Miss Henman carried on quietly talking to herself.

Mr. Marlow looked in the rear-view mirror. The kids were fit to burst. They were all sitting with their mouths and eyes tight shut, bright red cheeks puffed out like party balloons.

As for Queeny she was shaking with fear within her deep-fried shell. She could sense Ted in the car but couldn't see him or do anything about it.

They arrived at the vets.

"I'll go in with Miss Henman" said Mr Marlow "Ed you can lock the car up and make sure you do your laces up, you'll trip"

Ed looked down at his perfectly tied laces. His Dad winked. Ed nodded. As soon as Miss Henman was through the doors they erupted. Ed literally fell on the floor laughing. It took a couple of minutes to recover.

Inside Mr Marlow was taking control of the situation.

We have an emergency here he stated with some authority as they approached the reception. He carefully guided Miss Henman round a number of dogs lying on the floor with various bandages and the strange cone shaped collars they wear when they're injured. There were carry cases for cats too and a cage with very large parrot and a glass tank containing a snake.

"OK, said the receptionist, as you can see, we're very busy but I'll get one of the nurses to come and take a quick look. Can you tell me what happened?

"The b-b-b-batter, fell in batter"

The receptionist looked at Mr Marlow who did what he could to explain.

The nurse came in. She calmly looked through the eyeholes, tapped the hard casing, nodded and wrote a few notes down.

We'll soon get this sorted – take a seat and I'll get things prepared. I'll be back in two minutes.

They sat quietly. Mr Marlow was surprised how quiet it was with so many animals around. There was an occasional squawk, snuffle, or meow but otherwise it was calm.

Based on what you know about the affect Ted had on Tyson, Bullet and Queeny you've probably got a pretty good idea of what was about to happen.

The three kids took a deep breath and walked in together. For about five seconds there was complete silence. Every animal's eyes were fixed firmly on Ted. Then - total chaos.

Cats in their carry cases span round spitting and screeching like furry catherine wheels.

The parrot's feathers all fell out with the shock, leaving the poor bird wide eyed and naked on its perch.

The dogs all made for the same exit - the corridor leading to the treatment rooms. The ones wearing the head cones couldn't see and all ran into each other in a tangle of terriers, spaniels and labradoodles.

The nurses and the vets, hearing the commotion ran into the corridor and were bundled over by the petrified pets.

Mr Marlow glanced at Ted and began to realise what was going on.

"Miss Henman , I'll come back to get you and the cat in half an hour. I just need to take the kids home for their tea"

"But it isn't anywhere near teatime" replied Jess

"No but we need to get back" insisted Mr Marlow as he shepparded the kids towards the door.

As soon as they left, the waiting-room calmed down again. The clear up began as confused Vets and Nurses, and some of the pet owners, picked up chairs and swept up feathers. The only dog who hadn't run away was an elderly pug. His owner had a tight grip on him when the madness started. The only slight problem was that a number of the parrots longer feathers had dropped into his cone so he looked more like a furry flower vase.

By the time Mr Marlow returned it was pretty much back to normal. Apart from the parrot who's owner was complaining loudly that she had arrived with a beautiful blue and yellow healthy parrot who needed his claws clipped and was now the owner of a pale shivering naked lump which looked more like a small uncooked chicken.

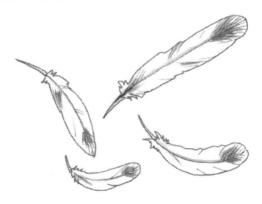

Chapter 12
Sports Day

Ted' first few days at school went by without any trouble.

Thursday was PE. It was a stunning Autumn day, so they were out on the school field.

Ed was pretty good at PE. He wasn't the fastest, but he had a good eye for a ball. He also won the standing long-jump in the school sports day.

With the next sports day a couple of weeks away they were trying out some of the events.

Miss Frost had a free period. She didn't think PE was a proper lesson but it was a lovely day, so she took her cup of tea and a doughnut and carefully dragged a chair out to the school field.

She sat near enough to Mr Wintergreen's class so that anyone watching thought she was interested in what they were doing but far enough away not to be disturbed by the sweaty oiks.

"OK Ed" said Mr. Wintergreen "show them your standing long jump. The class gathered on either side of him. A few of the kids couldn't see so well so they stood at the far end of the jump pit.

Ed put his toes to the line. Bent his legs a few times, swung his arms for extra momentum then leapt forward.

"Nice jump Ed" encouraged Mr Wintergreen, "let's see if your cousin can do as well as you"

Ted shrugged and stepped forward to the line. Ed joined Ben and Will at the end of the jump area to get a good view.

"Is he any good?". asked Ben

"No idea" Ed replied "we'll know soon enough"

Ted didn't do the same knee bending and arm swinging as Ed.

Instead he squatted down and staid still. He remained in that position for a few seconds - completely still. The kids began looking at each other quizzically. Mr. Wintergreen looked puzzled too. He was just about to check if Ted was OK when he launched forward.

Ben, Will and Ed stared upwards open mouthed as Ted's leap took him well clear of their heads. Unfortunately, the kids at the end of the pit had blocked Ted's view. As he got ready to land, he noticed Miss Frost who was taking a sip of her tea. It was too late to do anything.

Miss Frost was vaguely aware of a shadow but before she could look up Ted's heels clipped her shoulder.

The impact tipped her chair over backwards. As her legs flailed in the air the chair-leg tore through her tights and stuck right through and out of the other side just below her knee meaning she couldn't move her right leg. Fortunately, it had missed her leg completely

Tea had covered her glasses causing them to mist-up. As she fell, she squeezed the doughnut, squirting jam up her left arm.

There was a moment of silence. Mr Wintergreen ran forward. But he wasn't coming to help. He had his

tape measure in his hand. He's never seen a jump like it. He could be famous. He'd be interviewed on TV. The PE teacher who coached a world record holder.

As he got within a few meters of Miss Frost she let out a dreadful scream.

He dropped the tape measure but took a careful look at where Ted had landed so he could go back later to check the distance.

Chapter 13

999

Miss Frost couldn't move. Through steamy, tea covered specs she tried to evaluate what had happened to her.

She couldn't move her right leg which seemed to be hanging at a dreadful angle. Glancing at the red liquid running down her left arm she assumed she had been badly injured.

Mr Wintergreen stepped forward.

"Call an ambulance" screamed Miss Frost

"I, I, I ...... I don't think we need an ambulance" he stammered "let me just help you back up"

"Don't you dare touch me you stupid man.... I'm injured, call and ambulance"

As he fumbled for his mobile the school nurse came waddling across the field at top speed (top speed for Mrs Compress was about one mile an hour but she was doing her best and she was carrying the first aid kit)

"Are you OK?" she asked as she got closer

"Of course, I'm not OK" shouted Miss frost "I've broken my leg and cut my arm horribly, I need professional help – I don't want you amateurs coming anywhere near me"

"But, but, but... I could just help you up" Said Mrs Compress.

Miss Frost just screamed.

Mr Wintergreen looked at Mrs Compress as he waited for the emergency services to answer. They both shrugged their shoulders.

Three minutes later the sound of sirens could be heard; seconds later two paramedics came sprinting across the field.

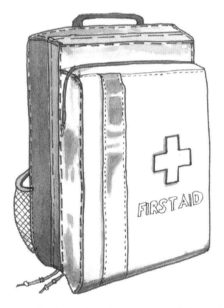

By now the whole school was watching the events unfold from their various classroom windows.

The paramedics knelt down. Where does it hurt?

"Are you serious?" whispered Miss Frost through gritted teeth

"Look at my leg!"

They looked.

"Let's get you up so we can take a better look"

One of the paramedics reached for her jam covered arm.

Mind that cut....hurry up I'm losing blood

"I think it's just jam madam" he said noticing the crushed remains of the doughnut.

They took a pair of scissors out of their bag to cut Miss Frost's tights and free her from the chair leg.

Spotting the scissors caused Miss Frost to faint.

When she came round a few seconds later she was sitting in the chair. She waited a moment, certain that she would feel dreadful pain, but nothing happened. One of the ambulance men was wiping the jam from her arm. The other was cleaning her glasses.

Mr. Wintergreen's entire class were rolling around helpless with laughter.

The paramedics were trying to remain professional.

"We had better take you for a checkup, you've had a nasty shock, but we don't think you've got any injuries.

They helped her up.

 She looked a sorry sight as she staggered across the field with a paramedic on each side. The tea had matted her hair and mixed with the jam to create a big pink stain on her white blouse. To make things worse she didn't realise that the remains of her tights were dragging behind her like sad tail.

It was, without doubt, the worst day of her life.

Chapter 14
Marshmallows

The following week on their way back from the park the Marlows stopped for a drink at the café on the high street. Even in the summer the kids loved a hot-chocolate in Coster-Lottabucks.

As usual there was a queue.

"Go find a table" said Mr Marlow.

The café was in an old higgledy-piggledy building, so it was a bit of a maze.

The kids glanced around – Jess pointed and started walking towards a table for four. Ed grabbed her and shook his head. Jess couldn't figure out what he was doing. The table was close and big enough. Using his head, he gestured beyond the table. There, at a table for two against the wall, sat Philbert Bland and Miss Frost. The kids did a u-turn and zig-zagged around the café. The only other free table was pretty close to Bland and Frost but a plant trough with a series of plastic trees in it meant they could sit without being seen.

After a few minutes Mr Marlow struggled through the café with a tray full of drinks.

"So, what was wrong with the table over there?"

"Nothing – we just liked this one better"

Mr Marlow distributed the hot chocolate, cream and marshmallows.

The kids tucked in

"Anything you'd like to say" he said.

"Thanks for the hot chocolate dad" chimed Jess and Ed. They all looked at Ted. He was sitting with his head on one side, eyes wide open.

The other three just shrugged and carried on with their drinks.

As they walked home Ted gestured to Ed and Jess to hold back a bit. "You OK?" asked Ed "you were a bit weird in there"

"I'm fine, I could hear Miss Frost talking to Philbert. They're planning something"

"What, like a trip to the science museum?"

"No something really big, something massive. Something which could affect thousands of people"

Ted looked serious.

"They think they've found a way to disrupt all of the mobile and wireless networks in the area"

Jess and Ed looked at each other and started firing questions.

"How will they do it?"

"Why are they doing it?"

 "When are they doing it?"

Ted held up his hands

"Whoa whoa whoa" he said "I don't know any of that. I just heard them say that's what they're going to do."

Chapter 15
Candyfloss

An hour later Philbert Bland and Miss Frost were standing in Philbert's massive garden shed. From the outside it looked like a fairly normal wooden shed - but inside it was different. He'd even dug down to give himself more space.

He and Miss Frost stood at the doorway looking down the steps. Philbert flicked the light switch.

There in the middle of the floor was a huge sheet covering something the size of a larger car.

They walked slowly down the steps and stood near the object. Philbert stepped forward and pulled the sheet back to reveal his masterpiece. Miss Frost looked and nodded with approval.

"Nice, very nice" she said, slowly and deliberately "Does it work?"

Philbert frowned, he was slightly offended. "Yes, yes it does"

What he had revealed looked like a massive candy-floss machine.

There was a reason for that. Philbert had got the idea when he was at the fair in the park. He watched as the guy on the stall popped the wooden stick into the vortex of spinning sugar, strand after strand building until it was just the right size for the customer.

Philbert stood watching for a long time.

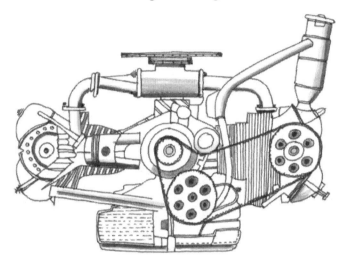

"D'you want one mate?" the stall holder called out after a while.

"Errr no, no thank you" replied Philbert

"Are you waiting for your kids then?"

"No, I, I don't have any - I'm just watching the machine"

"Well can you watch it from a bit further away – you're scaring the kids in the queue"

Philbert had seen enough. He turned to walk away and heard the candy floss man whisper "Weirdo".

 Philbert had created a sticky wireless wave. Other

signals were attracted to it. He could send little bursts of the sticky wireless out of his shed window. If you've ever been between the Chiltern Hills and the River Thames in Buckinghamshire and lost your phone signal for no obvious reason or your laptop or tablet suddenly dropped its connection it was probably Philbert's sticky wireless signal.

It only caused the signal to be lost for 20-30minutes but if he did it a few times a day he would always get a little more business as the Can Do Computer store sent him laptops which seemed to have a network connection problem.

Now with his candy-floss inspired machine he could really cause a problem.

Rather than just cause a temporary glitch he could suck all the signals from the town and cause chaos. He could pretty much name his price for fixing the problem.

Chapter 16
Spying

Ed, Ted and Jess were deciding what to do.

"We could find out more? If they really are planning something, we could stop them – it would be an adventure – we'd be like Scooby Doo and the gang" said Jess.

"Kind of" said Ed sarcastically – apart from the fact that there are three of us and four of them, we don't have the mystery machine or a massive talking dog"

Jess folded her arms and glowered at her brother.

"The thing is" said Ted "Jess is kind of right – we need to find out what they're doing – then we can tell Dad, or the police"

"We could follow him and spy on him – that would be pretty fun."

So, the following day they asked if they could go to the park.

They weren't too sure what a spy should have.

Ed had a ball of string and a small Swiss Army knife he used for fishing.

Ted had a torch – even though it was the middle of the day.

Jess had bought a large Scooby Doo soft toy.

They knew that Philbert's garden backed on to the long alley which led to the park. There was a tall wooden fence on either side of the path. It took them a while to figure out exactly which house was Philbert's but eventually they got to the part of the fence which they were sure had Philbert's garden on the other side. Checking up and down the path Ed put his eye to a hole low down on the fence.

"Wow- that's some shed he's got in there"

"Let me see. Let me see" whispered Jess excitedly "Find another hole" said Ed

"I can't reach up to the next one" she moaned.

"Stand on my back then".

Ed was on all fours with his eye pressed against the fence. Jess climbed up.

"Keep still Ed"

"Jess you're heavy, stop wobbling about"

Jess finally got her balance and looked through the hole. Just as she did the backdoor of the house began to open.

Ed moved backwards at some speed. As he did it sent Jess tumbling forward and crashing through the fence.

"Run !!!!"

Jess tumbled head-over-heels into the garden. She got up and made for the gap in the fence.

"Come on" shouted Ed.

As she got to the fence Ed and Ted ran – thinking she would be right behind them, but her lace was caught on the broken piece of fence.

The door was opening. Jess could hear voices.

Chapter 17
The Shed

Jess pulled back to free herself and realised she wouldn't get back through the fence before the owners of the voices were in the garden.

At the end of the shed was a pile of wood and a water butt. Luckily for Jess the grass was very long too. She rolled to the side and managed to get behind the water butt.

"I'm sure I heard something"

Jess recognised the voice and through a small gap between the water butt and the shed she saw the familiar shoes and brown tights belonging to Miss Frost.

Jess lay still. Her heart was beating so hard she was sure Miss Frost would hear it.

"Look at the fence" said Miss Frost – I told you I heard a crashing noise"

Philbert got to the fence "We can't have anyone looking through the fence today". He grabbed the broken piece of fence and held it up to the gap. "Quick, there's a tool box just inside the shed door, bring it and grab some bits of wood from that pile"

Jess moved back slightly and took a deep breath as Miss Frost grabbed at the pile of wood.

She heard the loud banging as Philbert hammered

as many nails in as he could. It wasn't a neat job but at least the hole was covered over.

Ed and Ted heard the banging too. They had run far enough to get round the corner of the alley and out of sight. They both lent against the fence gasping for air.

"C'mon Jess" called Ed "Jess?? Jess??"

The boys looked at each other.

"I thought she was right behind us"

"Me too – what was that banging?"

Suddenly the banging stopped.

"We need to go back and make sure she's OK".

They edged around the bend of the alley, staying tight in against the fence, peeping around the corner as they tip-toed along.

"This is it" whispered Ted.

"How did the fence get fixed so quickly?"

I hope Jess isn't on the other side. Ed crept up to a hole in the mended panel. At first the garden looked just the same he moved to look around. He could just see the white of Jess's trainers in the grass at the back of the shed and then he could make out other bits of clothing and finally her blond hair.

He whispered her name as loudly as he dared. She glanced around, not daring to speak

"Are you OK?" he asked

Jess gave a thumb up.

"Can you get out?"

Jess shrugged and shook her head, pointing to the shed to try to indicate that Philbert was inside.

Jess beckoned to the boys to come in. They looked at each other.

"OK" said Ted" at least we'll all be together, I'll lean against the fence you climb up and over. I can jump over no problem."

And that's what they did. Soon all three of them were crouched down at the back of the shed.

Chapter 18
Books

Jess Ed and Ted were all scared, but they also had the giggles! So for a few minutes they all couched in the grass with their hands over their mouths.

Then they heard voices. They glanced up.

There was an open window directly above them. They could hear Frost and Bland clearly.

"This window's open"

"Yes, the machine generates a huge amount of heat. When we start the process and I can pull the roof back fully to let the heat out; but for now we need to leave the window open.

We're nearly ready to go – in one hour's time we'll

start and pretty soon after that everyone around here will be in big trouble. A total communication black out. I'll have so many laptops to fix I can name my price."

"Yes"chipped in Miss Frost, "and the school won't be able to use any tablets or laptops for lessons – they'll all have to rely on proper old-fashioned teaching and I'm the only one who can do it properly. My final few terms will my best ever! The kids will have to use books – no more Googling stuff, no more presentations on PowerPoint no more fancy online number games. We'll have proper old style maths lessons, learning times-tables parrot fashion. In English lessons they'll read books made out of paper not on a Kindle and they'll write full sentences in their reports. No more LOLs no more smiley faces no more BTW and IKRs* I'll be an educational hero"

*I know right!

Miss Frost stood proudly for a moment with her fist clenched against her chest. In her mind it was the pose they would use to make a statue in her honour outside every school in the county.

The kids looked at each other – suddenly it was becoming clear why these two were making a plan together.

Nearby at Major Gunns house Molly, his granddaughter, was aware something was going on. Molly and her parents had arrived at the Major's house to have a two-week holiday. Molly and her family lived in Bristol. She and Jess were great friends even though they only saw each other a few times a year.

Molly had been unpacking her bag in the spare bedroom when she had heard loud banging. She had looked out of the window and seen Philbert banging nails into his fence. She was about to get back to unpacking when she noticed Jess hiding near the big shed.

She was worried. As she watched she had seen Ed and a kid she didn't recognise creep round the alley and stand by the fence. She had watched as Ed scrambled over and the was amazed as the other kid leapt straight over. She didn't want to get Jess into trouble, but she knew something was wrong. As she watched the Major had tapped on her door.

"How are you doing Molly? I have lemonade and doughnuts in the kitchen when you're ready"

Molly just stared out of the window.

"I'm OK, I think" she replied.

The Major opened the door and joined her at the window.

Molly pointed.

"What on earth is going on down there?" he said.

I've got no idea, but it doesn't look good does it? What should we do? They watched as Jess, Ed and Ted climbed through the window.

"That doesn't seem like the kind of thing that Jess would do" said the Major "I've been watching

Philbert for a while. There's definitely something strange going on in that shed. I don't want to get them into trouble, but we really should call the police"

Chapter 19
The Key

Meanwhile, next door to Philbert's house Miss Henman was having a strange day. Her cat, Queeny, hadn't been the same since the chip-shop incident and the trip to the vets which followed. In the end, having tried several cat-friendly shampoos they had only one answer; to shave the matted fur off completely. Queeny didn't look quite so cute without fur.

She looked like a big fat pink maggot with skinny legs and tufty ears which is a pretty hard thing to imagine. Miss Henman hadn't been out on her bike for a couple of weeks. She spent every day in her garden and as a result she had become aware of just how much noise Philbert Bland was making. For someone who was supposed to be fixing laptops there was a huge amount of banging, grinding and loud whirring.

Today, Queeny, who was just beginning to calm down a little, was acting very strangely. Miss Henman had no idea that Ted was in next door's garden but Queeny could sense it. The furless feline was cowering in the corner of the kitchen, hissing.

 Back in the shed Philbert and Miss Frost were still discussing their plan – "Right - I've switched the generator on - it takes a while to get up to speed – lets go and grab a cuppa – we'll come back in 15 minutes and get started.

Under the window at the back of the shed Ed, Ted and Jess were looking at each other. They were all scared and excited in equal measure. They were all thinking the same thing. Find a way over the fence, run home and persuade mum or dad to call the police or climb through the window and take a look at whatever was inside.

"We've got 15 minutes. Let's go in and take a quick look, then we can go back and tell the police exactly what we've seen" suggested Ed.

The window was only half open - Jess could just squeeze through. She wriggled in and opened the window fully, allowing Ed and Ted to climb in. They were in a small office filled with cabinets. Old desks and laptops. Dozens and dozens of them.

There was a door, half –open, through to the main part of the shed. Ed peeked through and gestured to the others to follow. They crept into the room

Ed took a few steps and winced as the board creaked beneath his feet.

Ted and Jess stopped and winced too.

Then to their horror they heard voices and the shed door began to open. They instinctively dropped down and shuffled back into the office room. The footsteps and voices got louder.

"I'll be back in a few seconds Miss Frost" they heard Philbert say "I'm not sure if I closed the window in the back room"

The kids knew they wouldn't all get back through the window in time. Fortunately, the room was so full of stuff it wasn't difficult to hide. They all crouched in silence.

 Philbert came into the room and walked over to the window

"That's odd" they heard him say to himself "I'm sure I only left this half open"

From her hiding place Jess saw him shrug, scratch his head and glance around the room. He pulled the window closed and then, to her dismay, he took a little key from the windowsill, locked the window and popped the key in his pocket.

He turned and left the room, closing the door behind him. They heard the click as he locked that too.

Once they were sure he'd gone they crept out of their hiding places.

"Now what?" asked Jess

They all looked round for a way out.

"We'll have to break the window" whispered Ted.

Jess was looking around thoughtfully for a better option. The wall which divided the room they were in from the main shed didn't go all the way up to the roof. There was a gap of about half a metre between the top of the wall and the angled roof.

"Ted, could you jump through there?" asked Jess.

"It's pretty high, and it'll have to be a pretty accurate leap to get through the gap...." he paused and looked up "......but I guess I'll have to give it a go"

Ted took a breath bent his legs and jumped. He splatted against the wall just below the gap and slid down to the floor.

"Epic fail" he groaned "rubbing the back of his head.

"You can do it" whispered Jess encouragingly.

He tried again – this time it was a perfect jump he reached the gap, perched on the wall and then dropped silently down.

The door key was still there. It took some jiggling, but he finally unlocked it. Jess and Ed slid quietly through.

Chapter 20
Scooby

The three of them stared at the center of the shed and all of them whispered "Wow" at the same time.

"It looks like something out of a sci-fi movie"

They were so amazed by the machine in front of them that they forgot where they were for a moment.

In silence they all took a couple of steps forward to get an even closer look. Jess still had her Scooby Toy with her, she held it tight. It made her feel a little less scared.

The silence was shattered by the sound of the door opening again and the voices of Bland and Frost.

"We may as well have our cup of tea in here" they heard Philbert Bland say. "You turn on the master switch to open the roof and then hit the red button to get the machine going, I'll bring over a table for our tea, then......................WHAT ARE YOU KIDS DOING!!!!!" He screamed.

The three kids stood frozen to the spot.

Miss Frost quickly closed the door behind her to prevent them escaping.

Philbert Bland spread his hands wide to block them. Ed and Jess went one way, Ted the other.

Miss Frost decided to get the machine going anyway.

"We can't let them out" shouted Philbert.

As Miss Frost pulled down the master switch and hit the red button there was a loud clunk and a grinding sound. The roof was opening - half of it was sliding back.

As a shaft of sunlight appeared through the roof Ted saw his chance.

He jumped vertically and grabbed onto a beam which formed part of the sliding roof.

Philbert Bland was desperate. Moving faster than he'd ever moved before he climbed a few steps to a platform on the edge of the machine.

Ted was setting himself to get through the gap, but the sliding roof was moving quickly and taking him towards Philbert Bland. As Ted's legs swung past- Philbert reached up and grabbed him round the waste. Ted wrapped his arms round the roof beam and held on with all his might. He and Philbert Bland were now a couple of meters above the machine.

Philbert looked down – "FLORENCE...TURN THE MACHINE OFF!!!!!! "he yelled

For a second the kids forgot how scared they were and looked at each other with a quizzical look. It never occurred to them that Miss Frost had a first name.

"WHAT?" Frost shouted back cupping her hand to her ear. The sound of the machine made it impossible to hear.

"A little help would be useful guys?" gasped Ted as he tried to support his own weight and Philbert's.

Jess made a dash towards Miss Frost who saw her coming and grabbed her by the wrist.

"Leave my sister alone" growled Ed and rugby tackled Miss Frost sending her and Jess tumbling to the floor.

Jess wrestled herself free.

Ted was still hanging above the machine with Philbert Bland clinging on.

Jess reached for the only thing she had with her – Scooby Doo. She grabbed it and threw it as hard as she could in the direction of Philbert.

As the toy flew over the machine it started to spin then suddenly it was sucked down onto the wire mesh guarding the opening of the machine.

"Thanks a lot" yelled Ted sarcastically "do something – this guy weighs a ton"

In the meantime, Miss Frost was trying to shove Ed away.

"Get off me - you horrible little twerp" she sneered – pushing him away with surprising force.

Philbert was losing his grip; he daren't let go. The only way was up.

He grabbed on to Ted's belt to heave himself up but instead he only succeeded in pulling Ted's jeans down slightly.

Ted's lizard tail was revealed. Philbert grabbed the tail

"What the heck........ what are you?"

Before he could say anymore the tail came off in his hand. He let go in horror sending the tail spiraling away. It hit the window and dropped to the floor"

Although Philbert had let go he wasn't falling - he

was whirling around like a hovering- spinning- top

Miss Frost reached for the control panel – finally realising that she must try to turn it off.

It was too late.

Philbert was going fuzzy. His head and hands were all out of focus. He was disappearing.

Suddenly his clothes whizzed off in all directions but Philbert had gone completely.

Miss Frost stood stunned with her hand on the master switch.

Meanwhile the Scooby Doo toy was being sucked hard against the wire mesh. His seams were loosening. They began to split. The beads which made up the filling shot through the gaps in the wire and into the machine. It started to make a dreadful sound.

There was a massive bang and a huge flash.

Dust filled the shed.

The kids didn't dare to move.

As the dust settled it revealed a chaotic scene.

The control panel had exploded. Miss Frost was still standing next to it with her hand on the switch. Her hair was sticking up in all directions, her face was black with soot and she was literally steaming.

Chapter 21
Noisy Neighbours

Next door Miss Henman had been listening with increasing annoyance as the craziness unfolded. She had no idea what was going on, but it was very noisy.

She had knocked on Philbert's front door to complain but there had been no reply. Philbert's mum, Mrs Bland, hated answering the door to anyone.

Eventually Miss Henman had called the police and was told that they were already on their way.

Sure enough the police arrived very quickly and to a very peculiar scene.

As the smoke and dust cleared, they could see a boy holding onto the rafters with his jeans pulled down revealing his bottom. A small girl was sitting on top of what looked like a monster food mixer with the remains of a Scooby toy while another boy was sitting on the floor pointing. He was pointing at a blackened and steaming old lady. Her hair was sticking out in all directions, her eyes were open wide, staring at the space above the machine. There was an eerie calm. Suddenly the lady shouted out "Detention!!!!!!" at the top of her voice. The police lady stepped a little closer "Madam... are you OK"

"Silence!" shouted Miss Frost.

"Madam, I'm a police officer.... Can you tell me what happened?"

Still staring straight ahead Miss Frost shouted again "How dare you ask me a question; I ask the questions! You're in detention and you'll go straight to the Head Teacher's office"

The police lady turned to her colleagues and made a circular motion with her finger at the side of her head to inform her colleagues that the lady was confused The officers helped Jess from the machine and Ted down from the rafters – luckily the kids were all fine.

There was a slight commotion at the door. Jess instantly recognised Molly's voice. Jess ran over and gave her a huge hug.

"Are you OK?" whispered Molly "we just arrived. I was unpacking; my bedroom window overlooks Philbert's garden. I could hear a dreadful noise and I thought I saw you through the shed window. I was calling Grandad to help and then I saw the police arrive"

One of the police officers took Molly to the side "Did you see what happened?"

"Not really" shrugged Molly "I'm Jess's' friend, I was looking out of the window up there - it looked like something was going on but I wasn't sure"

"OK" replied the officer "Can I take your details; you

may remember something important?"

By now the Major had arrived to check Molly was OK. "Molly is staying with me" reassured the Major "this is my address. We'll help if we can"

Molly looked around the room as the smoke and dust settled. She knew Ed but she soon noticed Ted who had successfully pulled his trousers back up. She nudged Jess and pointed "It's an awfully long story, I'll have to tell you later. It's a massive secret" whispered Jess.

On searching the shed the police found all of Philbert's plans and sketches. They found his shoes. They found his Power Rangers boxer shorts, his Minecraft Socks, His Batman T-shirt and his glasses. The one thing they could not find was Philbert Bland.

By now Mr and Mrs Marlow were on the scene and

soon after that Miss Bugle, a reporter from the local newspaper. Nothing much happened in Marlow. She was usually writing stories about pedestrian crossings, local fetes and missing dogs so this was pretty exciting. Mrs Marlow would not let her speak to the kids or take any pictures. It could make situation even more tricky if people asked too many questions about Ted, so Miss Bugle asked a police officer.

In the next day's edition of the paper she used a picture of the wrecked interior of the shed. The story told the public to be on the lookout for a stocky, bearded, shaggy haired, pale skinned, naked man in his late 50s who was on the run and potentially dangerous.

Actually, Philbert Bland wouldn't be spotted by anyone. He still existed but he existed in "The Cloud" and he loved it. He was a loosely connected set of protons. He messaged his Mum on her laptop to let her know he was OK. But he was more than OK. He could create all kinds of mischief. He would notice someone trying to download an app, wait until it was 98% complete and then break the connection with a swish of his virtual arm.

People buying tickets online for the latest boy band re-union would get to the very last box of the payment screen, full of excitement when "Sorry the website you are viewing is not responding, please press refresh"

Pretty soon Philbert began to soften his attitude. Instead of annoying everyone he realised how often he could help and that began to give him more satisfaction. He could cure computer viruses; he could spot hackers trying to steal passwords and stop them. He loved it.

Chapter 22

The next chapter

As for Miss Frost it was impossible to prove how involved she had been in the plan. They found her a place in the nearby "Marlow Home for Deranged Teachers" As you might imagine it was pretty full but she loved it. Thirty old teachers sitting in a big room which was designed to look like a big school staffroom. Some sat in silence rocking slightly from side to side. Occasionally one would jump up and shout "Quiet at the back!!" or "What do you mean the dog ate your homework!!??"

Miss Frost loved it - they had given her a small blackboard, a huge supply of chalk and an old-fashioned board-rubber. She taught an imaginary class and every now and then she clapped the board-rubber into her hand sending a satisfying cloud of chalk dust into the air. During the day, the buildup of dust gave her a strangely ghostly appearance, but she had never been happier.

Ed and Jess had seen what Ted could do. He was freakishly strong for his size. He could climb way quicker, run much faster and jump far higher than anyone. Mr. and Mrs. Marlow had realised what was going on too. But it was not just them. Major Gunn had been thinking about Ted ever since the incidents with the dogs, Tyson and Bullet, in the park. Major Gunn was a very clever man. He knew there was something odd about Ted's arrival and the affect he seemed to have on animals. He could not quite fit everything together as he had no idea of the full story.

The Major walked to the top of the stairs in his house, flicked a switch on the wall and the loft opened above him - a ladder quietly slid down. He climbed up into the loft above. It was not like a normal loft. It was a very smart office. In the middle was a "U" shaped desk with 3 large flat screens. The Major sat on the chair at the desk and tapped the password into his keyboard. He looked at the screens, scrolled the curser across a few images stroked his beard. After a few minutes, The Major stood up and started to walk around the office. He pulled on a small handle and opened a door. Behind it was a glass case. In the glass case were items of clothing. Gloves, leggings, balaclavas and jackets. In the last few years in the army the Major had overseen specialist military clothing. When he left the army, they had asked him to continue his research. Eventually they had ended the project but The Major still had the files and samples.

He was starting to form a plan in his head.

His thoughts were interrupted by the sound of Molly calling him.

"I'll be there in a second" he called out.

He quickly and quietly closed his office and made his way downstairs.

Molly was excited. She hadn't told Jess yet, but she was moving to Marlow. Her mum had got a great job nearby and they were all moving in with the Major while they looked for a house to live in.

As for Ed, Ted and Jess, they had solved a proper mystery and they all had a feeling that it would not be the last.

They didn't know it yet, but the Major was thinking along the same lines.

Printed in Great Britain
by Amazon